Pinkalicious™

Pink of Hearts

Victoria Kann

HARPER FESTIVAL
An Imprint of HarperCollinsPublishers

For the delightful Jessica D.
—V.K.

The author gratefully acknowledges
the artistic and editorial contributions
of Daniel Griffo and Natalie Engel.

HarperFestival is an imprint of HarperCollins Publishers.

Pinkalicious: Pink of Hearts
Copyright © 2011 by Victoria Kann, Inc.
PINKALICIOUS and all related logos and characters are trademarks of Victoria Kann, Inc. Used with permission.
Based on the HarperCollins book *Pinkalicious* written by Victoria Kann and Elizabeth Kann, illustrated by Victoria Kann
All rights reserved. Manufactured in China.
No part of this book may be used or reproduced in any manner whatsoever without
written permission except in the case of brief quotations embodied in critical articles and reviews.
For information address HarperCollins Children's Books,
a division of HarperCollins Publishers, 10 East 53rd Street, New York, NY 10022.
www.harpercollinschildrens.com

Library of Congress catalog card number: 2011927580
ISBN 978-0-06-198923-0

Book design by John Sazaklis
11 12 13 14 15   LEO   10 9 8 7 6 5 4 3 2 1
❖
First Edition

3 9082 12205 9465

vas Friday, art day at school.
Pushkin said he had a big treat for us.

"Monday is Valentine's Day. We're going to have a secret valentine exchange and party to celebrate!" Mr. Pushkin announced. "Everyone will pick someone's name out of a hat. Your homework is to make them the most spectacular valentine and then share it with them at the party!"

I almost jumped out of my seat. This party was made for me!
Valentine's Day is the most pinkerrific holiday of the year.

Mr. Pushkin passed around the hat. I was breathless with excitement. I looked at each of my classmates as they took their turns, trying to figure who had the slip of paper with my name, but no one peeked over at me onc

"Pinkalicious," said Mr. Pushkin, interrupting my search. "It's your turn to choose."

My hands shook as I reached for a slip of paper. When I opened it up, I saw my best friend's name written out in big block letters: ALISON.

"Yes!" I squealed as quietly as I could. This was shaping up to be the best party ever. Not only would I make Alison the most dazzling valentine, but I was sure to get a beautiful pink card in return.

That weekend, I got to work. I started cutting out pink hearts like crazy.

"Yuck," said Peter when he saw the mess I had made. "It looks like a pink-sty in here."

"I believe you mean it looks like a pink paradise," I said. "Do you want to help me, Peter? Do you think I need more hearts?"

With Peter's help, I finished the hearts in no time. Then I carefully wrote out HAPPY VALENTINE'S DAY, ALISON! in big letters and signed my name in cursive.

Then I turned the valentine over and sprinkled some special glitter all over the front of the card to make it sparkle and shine.

I even squirted a little pink perfume to give it that extra-special touch.
"There," I said to Mommy and Daddy when I was all done. "What do you think?"
"Pinkturesque," said Mommy.
"Valentinalicious," said Daddy.

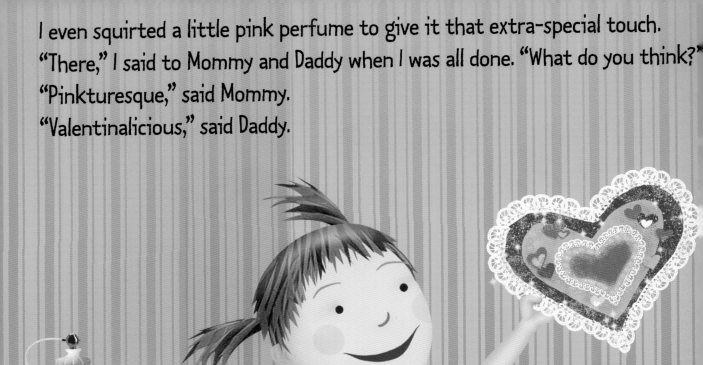

There was no doubt about it. Alison was going to love her card.

That night, with my perfect valentine tucked safely away in my backpack
started to imagine the card my secret valentine was making for *me*. I pictur
myself at the party, carefully opening up a pink-and-gold envelope with a
beautiful pink-and-lace valentine inside.

my," I'd gush. "Pink is always perfect, but it's even better on a valentine!"
at night I fell asleep with a huge smile on my face.

At the party the next day, I had lots of fun eating cupcakes and heart-shaped cookies, but I couldn't stop thinking about the secret valentine exchange. I knew that somewhere in the art room was a one-of-a-kind valentine with my name on it. I couldn't wait to see it.

At last, Mr. Pushkin passed out the envelopes one by one. Alison got hers first. When she opened the card I made for her, her face lit up. "Oh, Pinkalicious," she said. "This is the nicest valentine anyone has ever given me!" I gave her a quick squeeze.

Then Mr. Pushkin handed me a plain white envelope. It had my name printed on it, but it looked nothing like what I had imagined. I opened it up slowly.

Inside was a regular piece of paper, folded in half, with one very small pink heart on the cover. On the back was the name of the person who had made it for me: Alison.

I couldn't believe it. I had worked so hard on my valentine for Alison, and all I got in return was something plain and simple. It looked like it had taken her no time at all to make it. My feelings were so hurt, I didn't know what to do.

I turned around so that Alison wouldn't see me. As I tried to move away, the card slipped out of my hand and fell open on the floor. That's when I noticed something inside that I hadn't seen before.

It was a poem that Alison had written for me.

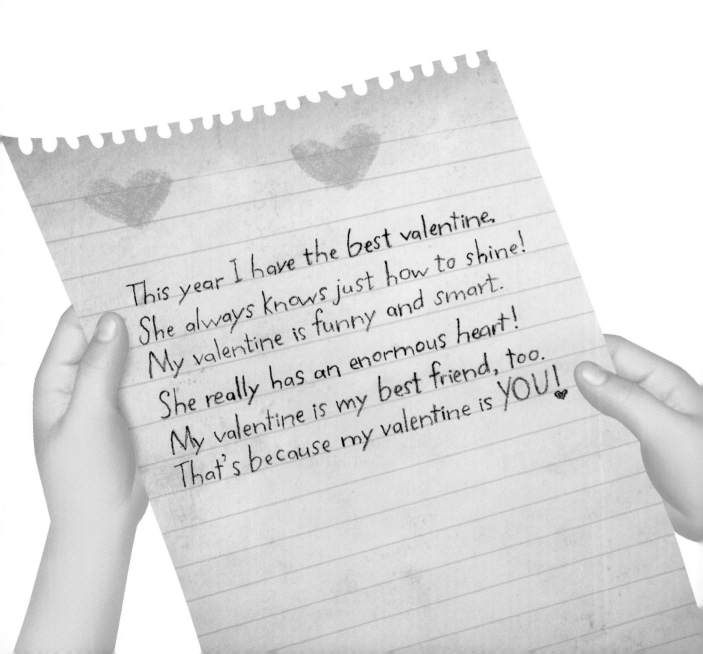

This year I have the best valentine,
She always knows just how to shine!
My valentine is funny and smart,
She really has an enormous heart!
My valentine is my best friend, too.
That's because my valentine is YOU!

"Wow," I said. No one had ever written something that sweet to me before. I held the card tight against my heart.

It was the best valentine I had ever gotten.